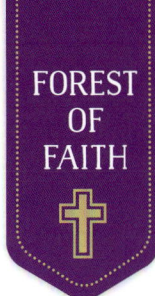

God's Very GOOD PLAN

A Christmas Story about Trusting God

Written by Abigail Gehring Lawrence and William Lawrence

Illustrations by Estelle Corke

New York, New York

Little Badger looked at the advent calendar. There were six days until Christmas, which meant seven days until the snow sculpture contest on the Great Meadow. He was determined to win this year.

To practice, he built a giant snow rabbit, a turtle, a snow train, and even a *full* nativity scene with Mary, Joseph, baby Jesus, and all the barn animals.

Little Bunny and Little Squirrel stopped by on their way to go sledding. "Wow," said Little Bunny. "You're really good!"

More friends stopped by to admire his work the next day and the day after that. Often, friends asked if he wanted to take a break to play, but he never did.

Soon it was the day before Christmas, and all the forest friends were gathering for a giant snowball fight. "Please come," begged Little Badger's younger sister. "You're the best snowball maker!" Little Badger shook his head. He wanted to keep working on his sculptures.

"Go with your sister," said Mama Badger. "She misses playing with you and so do your friends."

Reluctantly, Little Badger trudged through the woods with Sister Badger.

At first, he could only think about his snow sculptures, but soon he got swept up in the fun. He could pack snowballs faster and better than anyone else.

He decided to make a quick dash across the pond to the big rock—the perfect fortress. As he was racing over the ice, his paws went out from under him, and he slid right into the rock. *Boom!*

"Yow!" he cried out.

"Are you ok?" Sister Badger hurried over to him, her eyes worried.

Little Badger was crying now. "My wrist," he said, holding it with the opposite paw.

His forest friends helped him up and walked him home, where Mama Badger hugged him and gave his wrist a close look.

"We need to get it checked out," she said.

The doctor confirmed that Little Badger's wrist was broken. He sent him home with a bandage and instructions to come back in a few days when the swelling had gone down.

"What about the sculpture contest?" cried Little Badger.

"I'm sorry, friend. You must not use that paw, or you'll make it much worse," said the doctor.

That night, as Mama Badger tucked him in, he blurted out, "Why did God let me break my wrist? You told me to go with Sister, and I was trying to do the right thing!"

Mama didn't answer right away. She just waited.

Eventually, Little Badger said shyly, "Mama, I think I'm mad at God."

"It's ok to feel mad," answered Mama softly. "Just remember, God loves you, and He's always good. Why don't you tell God how you *feel*? Then we'll pray that your wrist heals really *fast!*"

In the morning, his wrist hurt even more. "Mama!" said Little Badger as they sat down for Christmas breakfast. "God didn't heal my wrist really fast. Doesn't He want to help me?"

"It's ok to feel confused," said Mama. "Just remember, God loves you, and He's always good. But I'm sorry it hurts right now. Let's open gifts to take your mind off it."

Little Badger and his sister each had a present wrapped in red- and gold-striped paper. Little Badger got a brand new shovel... which would have been perfect for the contest.

As Mama was picking up the wrapping paper, she noticed he was sniffling quietly. She stopped to give him a hug.

"Mama," Little Badger said, his tears coming fast now. "I really wanted to win the snow sculpture contest!"

"It's ok to be sad," said Mama. "God loves you, and I promise He wants what's best for you, even if it doesn't feel like it right now.

Sometimes we don't understand God's plans until much later."

"You know," she said, sitting down beside him, "I bet Mary was confused when she learned she was pregnant with Jesus. And I wouldn't be surprised if she was a little angry when God didn't provide a nicer place to have the baby. And I am sure she was very sad when Jesus died! It probably wasn't until later that she really understood God's beautiful plan."

The next day, Little Badger's family hiked along the trail to the Great Meadow to watch the snow sculpture contest. Little Badger dragged behind them, feeling sad and grumpy.

Mama and Papa and Sister were talking and didn't notice as Little Badger got farther and farther behind. Soon his family was out of sight, but he didn't care.

Alone in the woods, he thought he heard a squeaking noise. He paused. There it was again. Curious, he plodded over to the bank. "Help!" It was Little Mouse. The ice had broken open, and Little Mouse was clinging to the edge, about to slip in!

Little Badger hurried down the bank, grabbed a long stick with his good hand, and thrust it toward Little Mouse. "Grab on!" he shouted. Little Mouse did, and Little Badger pulled him to safety. He wrapped his soft scarf around the shivering mouse.

"Thank you," said Little Mouse, his voice shaking. "You saved me." As Little Badger rubbed Little Mouse up and down to warm him, Little Mouse explained, "I thought the ice was thicker. You came just in time."

Little Badger carried Little Mouse to the contest where he found Mr. and Mrs. Mouse. They'd been looking frantically for Little Mouse. They'd even been making announcements over the loud speaker and were beginning to organize a search party.

Mama put an arm around him as they walked.

"I don't think God ever likes it when we're hurting," she said. "But He's always with us, and we can always trust Him with our *feelings*. Sometimes when we're hurting or weak, God uses us in especially mighty ways!"

Little Badger thought about this as they walked along the trail lined with snowy pine trees. Silently, he prayed, "God, thank you *for* using me to help Little Mouse today. Help me to remember you're always good, and you always have a good plan."

Copyright © 2025 by Abigail Gehring Lawrence and William Lawrence
Illustrations by Estelle Corke

All rights reserved. No part of this book may be reproduced in any manner without the express written consent of the publisher, except in the case of brief excerpts in critical reviews or articles. All inquiries should be addressed to Good Books, 307 West 36th Street, 11th Floor, New York, NY 10018.

Good Books books may be purchased in bulk at special discounts for sales promotion, corporate gifts, fund-raising, or educational purposes. Special editions can also be created to specifications. For details, contact the Special Sales Department, Good Books, 307 West 36th Street, 11th Floor, New York, NY 10018 or info@skyhorsepublishing.com.

Good Books is an imprint of Skyhorse Publishing, Inc.®, a Delaware corporation.

Visit our website at www.goodbooks.com.

10 9 8 7 6 5 4 3 2 1

Manufactured in China, 2025
This product conforms to CPSIA 2008

Library of Congress Cataloging-in-Publication Data is available on file.

Cover design by Kai Texel
Cover illustration by Estelle Corke

Good Books ISBN: 978-1-68099-969-3
Scholastic ISBN: 978-1-966995-03-6
Ebook ISBN: 978-1-68099-980-8